Dear Parent:
Your child's love of reading starts here!

Every child learns to read in a different way and at his or her own speed. Some go back and forth between reading levels and read favorite books again and again. Others read through each level in order. You can help your young reader improve and become more confident by encouraging his or her own interests and abilities. From books your child reads with you to the first books he or she reads alone, there are I Can Read Books for every stage of reading:

SHARED READING
Basic language, word repetition, and whimsical illustrations, ideal for sharing with your emergent reader

BEGINNING READING
Short sentences, familiar words, and simple concepts for children eager to read on their own

2 **READING WITH HELP**
Engaging stories, longer sentences, and language play for developing readers

3 **READING ALONE**
Complex plots, challenging vocabulary, and high-interest topics for the independent reader

4 **ADVANCED READING**
Short paragraphs, chapters, and exciting themes for the perfect bridge to chapter books

I Can Read Books have introduced children to the joy of reading since 1957. Featuring award-winning authors and illustrators and a fabulous cast of beloved characters, I Can Read Books set the standard for beginning readers.

A lifetime of discovery begins with the magical words **"I Can Read!"**

Visit www.icanread.com for information on enriching your child's reading experience.

HARP29131

Library of Congress catalog card number: 2012956498
ISBN 978-0-06-221003-6

Book design by John Sazaklis

17 18 SCP 10 9 8 7 ❖ First Edition

I Am Aquaman

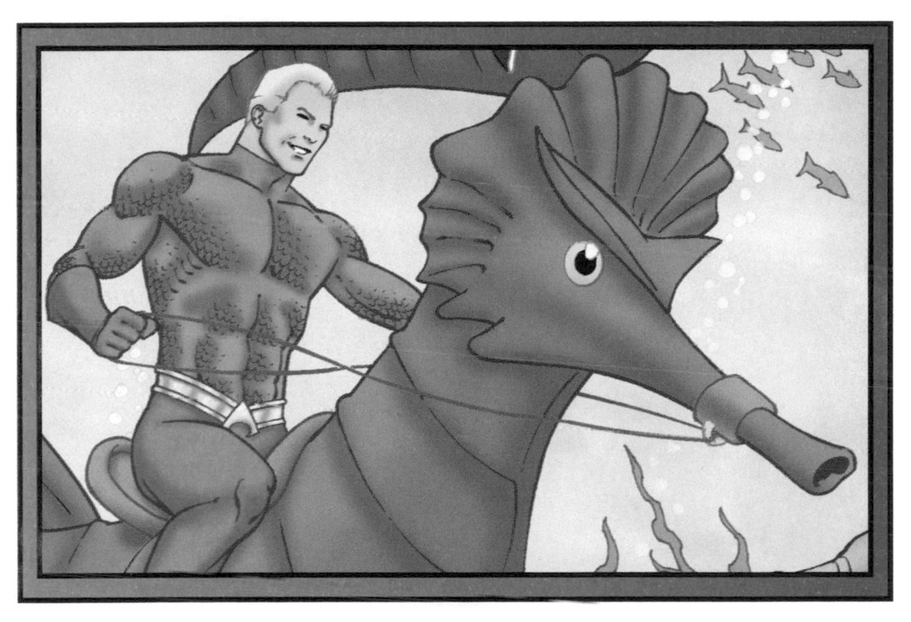

by Kirsten Mayer
pictures by Andy Smith
colors by Brad Vancata

AQUAMAN created by Paul Norris

HARPER
An Imprint of HarperCollins*Publishers*

Under the sea is a land
called Atlantis.
Aquaman and Mera
are king and queen of Atlantis.
Aquaman protects the sea
and also helps humans on land.
He is on a team of super heroes
called the Justice League.

The other heroes are coming
to see Atlantis and meet Mera.
Aquaman greets Green Lantern,
Wonder Woman, Batman, and Superman
on the surface of the water.
"Hello, friends! Welcome to the sea!
I have sea horses for you to ride."
The sea horses poke their heads out.

"I can't wait to meet Mera,"

says Wonder Woman.

"And to see your castle,"

says Superman.

"What sort of power source
do you use under the sea?"
asks Batman.
Aquaman chuckles.
"Come see for yourselves!"

“Here, this will help.”
Green Lantern uses his power ring
to create face masks for the heroes
so they can all go underwater.
Aquaman can breathe underwater
and Superman can hold his breath.
Everyone rides sea horses down
to the bottom of the ocean.
They enter the city of Atlantis.

Aquaman points out Mercy Reef
and the hydropower plant.
The group gets off the sea horses
and swims into a golden castle.

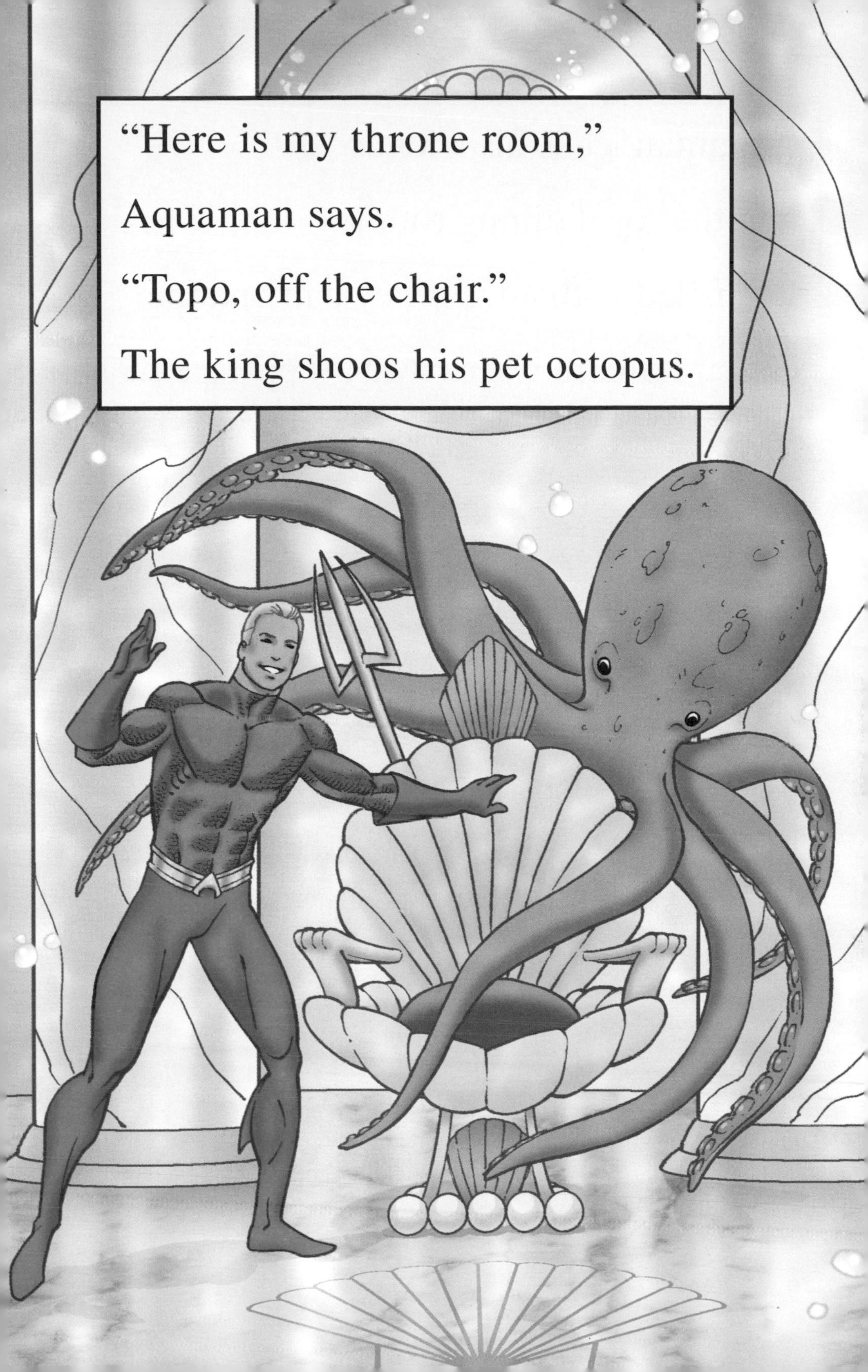
"Here is my throne room,"
Aquaman says.
"Topo, off the chair."
The king shoos his pet octopus.

Aquaman leads his friends

into the royal dining room.

It is filled with air, so they can breathe.

Green Lantern waves away their face masks.

"Welcome, everyone," says Mera.
"Arthur has told me so much
about each of you."
They all sit at a large table
covered with lots of delicious food.

Topo swims out to play
with his friends.
A dark shape swoops by.
It is Aquaman's enemy
Black Manta!

He is with King Shark
and his army of sharks.

In the dining room,
Aquaman drops his fork.
"We are under attack!"
he cries.

"How do you know?"
asks Superman.
"Topo and the dolphins—
I can hear them in my mind,"
says the king.

The heroes jump to their feet.
Wonder Woman says,
"We will help defend your home.
Hal, face masks please."
Green Lantern gives them face masks.
The team jumps into the water
and swims out to face the enemy.

Black Manta arrives.
He swims out of his ship
in his diving suit and helmet.
"I will be king now,"
he says to Aquaman.
"My buddy and his sharks
will take care of your friends."

Green Lantern uses his ring
to form a big fishing net.
Queen Mera has powers, too.

Mera controls the water currents
and forces the fish toward her friend.
"Catch!" she yells to Green Lantern.
He closes the net around the sharks.

King Shark tries to bite
Superman with his big teeth.
He punches the shark on the nose!

"Here's the biggest catch of the day!" Superman says to Green Lantern as the shark sails right into the net.

Black Manta fires
laser rays from his helmet.
Wonder Woman deflects the rays
with her silver bracelets.
Aquaman fights back
with his mighty trident.
"I rule Atlantis, Black Manta!"
he commands. "No one else!"

Batman gets into Manta's ship.
He zooms by and scoops up the foes.
Then Batman jumps out of the ship
and swims to his friends.
Aquaman forms a whirlpool
and sends the scoundrels far away.
The super heroes cheer.
Atlantis is safe once again!

Aquaman says,
"Thanks to all of you,
we showed Black Manta there is
only one King of the Seas.
I am Aquaman!"